何 不 浅 尝 辄 止
joy of first glimpse

我今天便要欢笑，今日转瞬即逝，我绝不为任何事等待。

美即是真，真即是美。

爱情像丛野蔷薇，
友谊像棵冬青树。

I wandered lonely as a cloud.

做一朵花，
在阳光下微微颔首。

你的刺是你最出色的地方。

一想起你，我就割伤了自己。

我仿佛一朵孤飞的流云，
在山谷之间缈缈游荡。

四月，它从山上走下，像个傻瓜，
胡言乱语，撒散鲜花。

Beauty is truth,
truth beauty.

你是呼喊，我就是回应；
你是许愿，我就是显灵；
你是夜晚，我就是白昼。

让你的笑容如翩翩波光，除了快乐再无所用。

我在世间游荡，
并邀我的灵魂同往。

Oh! To be a flower,
Nodding in the sun.

图书在版编目（CIP）数据

没有人是一座孤岛：治愈系现代诗 /（英）威廉·华兹华斯等著；李小蕾译 . -- 南京：江苏凤凰文艺出版社 , 2023.7（2025.4 重印）

（浅尝诗丛）

ISBN 978-7-5594-7679-1

Ⅰ.①没… Ⅱ.①威…②李… Ⅲ.①诗集 – 英国 – 现代 Ⅳ.① I561.25

中国国家版本馆 CIP 数据核字 (2023) 第 067046 号

没有人是一座孤岛：治愈系现代诗

（英）威廉·华兹华斯等 著　李小蕾 译

出 版 人	张在健
责任编辑	王娱瑶　徐　辰
特约编辑	韩馨雨
装帧设计	徐芳芳
责任印制	刘　巍
出版发行	江苏凤凰文艺出版社
	南京市中央路 165 号，邮编：210009
出版社网址	http://www.jswenyi.com
印　　刷	江苏凤凰新华印务集团有限公司
开　　本	880 毫米 ×1230 毫米　1/32
印　　张	6
字　　数	100 千字
版　　次	2023 年 7 月第 1 版　2025 年 4 月第 2 次印刷
标准书号	ISBN 978-7-5594-7679-1
定　　价	42.00 元

江苏凤凰文艺版图书凡印刷、装订错误，可向出版社调换，联系电话 025-83280257

浅尝诗丛

没有人是一座孤岛
治愈系现代诗
·中英双语·

[英]威廉·华兹华斯 等 著
凤凰诗歌出版中心 编　李小蕾 译

CONTENT 目录

Emily Dickinson

[美国] 艾米莉·狄金森

002　Hope Is the Thing with Feathers
003　希望

004　I Dwell in Possibility—
005　我栖居在可能性中

006　Dawn
007　破晓

008　Snow Flakes
009　雪花

010　The Mushroom is the Elf of Plants—
012　蘑菇是植物中的精灵

014　Like Some Old Fashioned Miracle
015　像某个古老的奇迹

Robert Frost

[美国] 罗伯特·弗罗斯特

018　The Road Not Taken
020　未选的道路

022　A Vantage Point
023　有利的位置

024　Stopping by Woods on a Snowy Evening
025　雪夜林边逗留

026　Dust of Snow
027　雪尘

028　The Pasture
029　牧场

Thomas Hardy
[英国] 托马斯·哈代

032　The Fallow Deer At the Lonely House
033　孤宅前的麋鹿

034　The Caged Thrush Freed and Home Again (Villanelle)
036　笼中的画眉获释返家（维拉内拉）

038　To Flowers From Italy in Winter
039　致严冬里的意大利花儿

040　Song of Hope
042　希望之歌

John Keats
[英国] 约翰·济慈

046　Ode on a Grecian Urn
049　希腊古瓮颂

052 Stanzas
054 诗节

056 To My Brothers
057 致我的兄弟们

058 A Thing of Beauty (Endymion)
060 美的事物（恩底弥翁）

D. H. Lawrence

[英国]戴维·赫伯特·劳伦斯

064 Dream-Confused
066 迷乱的梦

068 A White Blossom
069 一朵白色的花

070 Bei Hennef
072 在汉尼夫近郊

074 Green
075 绿

076 Butterfly
078 蝴蝶

Amy Lowell

[美国] 艾米·洛威尔

082 At Night
083 在夜晚

084 Sea Shell
085 贝壳

086 Dreams
087 梦

088 To A Friend
089 致一位友人

090　The Crescent Moon
091　新月

Claude McKay

[美国]克劳德·麦凯

094　After the Winter
095　冬季过后

096　Romance
098　浪漫

100　To One Coming North
101　致来到北方的人

102　I Shall Return
103　我会回来

104　Courage
105　勇气

Rabindranath Tagore

[印度] 罗宾德拉纳特·泰戈尔

108 Gitanjali 35
109 《吉檀迦利》第 35 首

110 Keep me fully glad... II
111 让我满心欢喜…… 2

112 The Gardener 85
113 《园丁集》第 85 首

114 Playthings
115 玩具

116 Song VII (Sing the song of the moment...)
118 歌 7（唱此刻的歌……）

Sara Teasdale

[美国] 萨拉·提斯黛尔

120　Leaves
121　叶子

122　The Answer
123　答案

124　Winter Stars
125　冬日的星

126　I Thought of You
127　我想起了你

128　The Voice
130　声音

Walt Whitman

[美国]沃尔特·惠特曼

134 On the Beach at Night Alone
136 独自在夜晚的海滩上

137 Beginning My Studies
138 开始我的研究

139 Music
140 音乐

141 Weave in, Weave in, My Hardy Life
142 编织进来吧,编织进来吧,我艰辛的生活

143 Song of Myself 1
145 自我之歌 1

146 By Broad Potomac's Shore
147 宽阔的波托马克河岸边

William Wordsworth
[英国]威廉·华兹华斯

150　I Wandered Lonely as a Cloud
152　我仿佛一朵孤飞的流云

154　A Complaint
155　哀怨

156　I Travelled among Unknown Men
157　我在陌生的人群中孤独穿行

158　Most Sweet it is
159　最为甜蜜的事情

160　It is a Beauteous Evening, Calm and Free
161　那是一个美丽的夜晚,静谧而自由

William Butler Yeats

[爱尔兰] 威廉·巴特勒·叶芝

164　When You Are Old
165　当你迟暮

166　The Lake Isle of Innisfree
167　茵尼斯弗利岛

168　The Travail of Passion
169　受难

170　Down by the Salley Gardens
171　漫步柳园

172　The Cat and the Moon
174　猫与月亮

Emily Dickinson
[美国] 艾米莉·狄金森
1830—1886

狄金森出生于19世纪的美国,她被誉为公元前7世纪萨福以来西方最杰出的女诗人。她一生都过着神秘的、隐居般的安静日子,生前发表过的诗歌不足10首。大部分动人的诗篇都被锁在盒子里,直到她去世数年之后才被发现。她与惠特曼一起,被称为美国现代派诗歌的先驱。她在迷人的孤独感里,倾听着世界的脉搏,描画着女性的灵魂。

Hope Is the Thing with Feathers

Hope is the thing with feathers
That perches in the soul,
And sings the tune without the words,
And never stops at all,

And sweetest in the gale is heard;
And sore must be the storm
That could abash the little bird
That kept so many warm.

I've heard it in the chillest land,
And on the strangest sea;
Yet, never, in extremity,
It asked a crumb of me.

希 望

希望披着羽毛
居于灵魂的深处,
哼着无词的曲调,
从未有过停止。

最欢喜莫过于在狂飙中忽闻其声;
风暴对此一定恼羞成怒
本可将鸟儿逼到绝路
但希望给予它温暖无数。

我曾在最寒冷的陆地上听闻它,
也曾在最诡谲的海洋上感受它,
然而,即使在最困窘的境地,
希望也不曾索要我面包屑一粒。

I Dwell in Possibility —

I dwell in Possibility —
A fairer House than Prose —
More numerous of Windows —
Superior — for Doors —

Of Chambers as the Cedars —
Impregnable of eye —
And for an everlasting Roof
The Gambrels of the Sky —

Of Visitors — the fairest —
For Occupation — This —
The spreading wide my narrow Hands
To gather Paradise —

我栖居在可能性中

我栖居在可能性中——

比散文更美的居所——

拥有更多的窗子——

还有更棒的——入口——

雪松制成的内室——

肉眼可见的坚固——

为了屋顶的耐久——

与天空拼出复折的图形——

优雅迷人的——客人——

要来——寒舍下榻——

我张开小小的双手——

去把乐园相拥——

Dawn

When night is almost done,
And sunrise grows so near
That we can touch the spaces,
It's time to smooth the hair

And get the dimples ready,
And wonder we could care
For that old faded midnight
That frightened but an hour.

破　晓

黑夜就要逝去，
太阳触手可及
在我们能摸到天地的时刻，
何不将一头青丝捋齐。

绽放出如花笑颜，
是否会计较之前
那仅仅持续了片刻的恐惧
来自一个衰老褪色的夜间。

Snow Flakes

I counted till they danced so

Their slippers leaped the town —

And then I took a pencil

To note the rebels down —

And then they grew so jolly

I did resign the prig —

And ten of my once stately toes

Are marshalled for a jig!

雪 花

我细数着直到它们舞姿疯狂

它们的拖鞋在镇子里踢踏游荡——

然后我拿起一支笔

记录这些反叛者的模样——

它们变得如此欢腾

我也扔掉了清高的气场——

我那十个曾经老实的脚趾

被带领着感受吉格舞的嚣张!

The Mushroom is the Elf of Plants—

The Mushroom is the Elf of Plants—
At Evening, it is not
At Morning, in a Truffled Hut
It stop opon a Spot

As if it tarried always
And yet it's whole Career
Is shorter than a Snake's Delay—
And fleeter than a Tare—

'Tis Vegetation's Juggler—
The Germ of Alibi—
Doth like a Bubble antedate
And like a Bubble, hie—

I feel as if the Grass was pleased
To have it intermit—
This surreptitious Scion
Of Summer's circumspect.

Had Nature any supple Face

Or could she one contemn—

Had Nature an Apostate—

That Mushroom — it is Him!

蘑菇是植物中的精灵

蘑菇是植物中的精灵——
一过傍晚就无影无踪
到了清晨,支起松露的小屋
它总在某地停留驻足

仿佛它总是如此逗留
其实它生命的全部
比一条小蛇的游弋还短暂——
比一棵稗草的衰败还飞快——

它是植物里的魔法师——
玩转不在场证明的菌子——
就像泡沫般抢先登场
又如泡沫般匆匆消亡——

我感觉草地十分乐于
让蘑菇做片刻的休息——
夏日私生的孩童
会将它悉心留意。

若自然有一张讨好的面庞

或是一副嫌弃的模样——

若自然有一位叛徒——

就是它!就是那蘑菇!

Like Some Old Fashioned Miracle

Like Some Old fashioned Miracle
When Summertime is done—
Seems Summer's Recollection
And the Affairs of June

As infinite Tradition
As Cinderella's Bays—
Or Little John — of Lincoln Green—
Or Blue Beard's Galleries—

Her Bees have a fictitious Hum—
Her Blossoms, like a Dream—
Elate us — till we almost weep—
So plausible — they seem—

Her Memories like Strains — Review—
When Orchestra is dumb—
The Violin in Baize replaced—
And Ear — and Heaven — numb—

像某个古老的奇迹

像某个古老的奇迹

当夏日悄然逝去——

似乎夏天的回忆

和六月的故事

将作为无尽的传说

将作为灰姑娘的枣红马——

抑或林肯绿的——小约翰——

抑或蓝胡子的美术馆——

她的蜜蜂有着虚拟的叫声——

她的花朵,就像梦境——

让我们狂喜,直至喜极而泣——

它们似乎,如此真诚——

她的记忆仿佛乐曲的——复歌——

在乐队静默的时刻——

小提琴也放回琴盒——

耳朵,以及天堂,都失去知觉——

Robert Frost
[美国] 罗伯特·弗罗斯特
1874—1963

弗罗斯特是美国家喻户晓的诗人,曾四次获得普利策诗歌奖。他的作品中常常萦绕着新英格兰故土的乡村风景,极具生活气息和人生哲理。他86岁那年,受邀在肯尼迪总统的就职典礼上朗诵诗歌。

The Road Not Taken

Two roads diverged in a yellow wood,
And sorry I could not travel both
And be one traveller, long I stood
And looked down one as far as I could
To where it bent in the undergrowth;

Then took the other, as just as fair,
And having perhaps the better claim,
Because it was grassy and wanted wear;
Though as for that the passing there
Had worn them really about the same,

And both that morning equally lay
In leaves no step had trodden black.
Oh, I kept the first for another day!
Yet knowing how way leads on to way,
I doubted if I should ever come back.

I shall be telling this with a sigh

Somewhere ages and ages hence:

Two roads diverged in a wood, and—

I took the one less travelled by,

And that has made all the difference.

未选的道路

两条道路在金色的树林分离，
可惜我无法同时将其踏遍
作为旅人，我长久地原地伫立
极目远眺，目之所及
灌木丛的深处，一条消失不见；

随后我选了另一条，也不无道理，
或许有着更加充分的考量，
只因它芳草萋萋、无比沉寂；
尽管从留下的足迹分析
两条道路都曾有脚步飞扬。

那天清晨它们并排躺着
叶落满地但未经洗礼。
哦，待我来日再选他路！
然而心下清楚道路连着道路，
我怀疑我能否找回原地。

在多年以后的某个地方

我会一声长叹,将往事提起:
两条道路在林中分离,而我——
我取了更加冷僻的那个选项,
从此生活就变了模样。

A Vantage Point

If tired of trees I seek again mankind,
Well I know where to hie me—in the dawn,
To a slope where the cattle keep the lawn.
There amid lolling juniper reclined,
Myself unseen, I see in white defined
Far off the homes of men, and farther still,
The graves of men on an opposing hill,
Living or dead, whichever are most to mind.

And if by noon I have too much of these,
I have but to turn on my arm, and lo,
The sun-burned hillside sets my face aglow
My breathing shakes the bluet like a breeze,
I smell the earth, I smell the bruised plant,
I look into the crater of the ant.

有利的位置

倘若厌倦了树林我会再次把人迹寻觅，
我知道应该奔赴哪里——到了早上，
去往青青的山坡，那里遍地牛羊。
在悠闲的刺柏树间小憩，
我隐遁不见，却能望见
远处人们白色的家园，和更远的地方，
对面山上人们的墓地，
活着或死去，不过是灵魂的印记。

如果到了午间我已经饱览了这些，
我只需转过我的臂膀，看哪，
阳光炙烤的山坡让我的脸颊发烫
我的呼吸像清风吹拂着蓝花草，
我闻到了泥土，闻到了植物的心伤，
我的目光向蚂蚁的洞穴张望。

Stopping by Woods on a Snowy Evening

Whose woods these are I think I know.
His house is in the village though;
He will not see me stopping here
To watch his woods fill up with snow.

My little horse must think it queer
To stop without a farmhouse near
Between the woods and frozen lake
The darkest evening of the year.

He gives his harness bells a shake
To ask if there is some mistake.
The only other sound's the sweep
Of easy wind and downy flake.

The woods are lovely, dark and deep,
But I have promises to keep,
And miles to go before I sleep,
And miles to go before I sleep.

雪夜林边逗留

树林的主人我了然于胸,
然而他的住所却在村落;
他不会看到我逗留林边,
望着他的树林白雪飘落。

我的小马一定觉得困惑,
半途停下周围并无农舍。
此刻在树林和冰湖之间
适逢一年里最深的夜色。

它轻轻摇动身上的佩铃
似在抱怨还有问题不明。
林子里唯一给予的回答
只是微风轻送雪片飘零。

这片树林优美且又幽深,
然而我有承诺尚在心头,
安歇前有长长的路要走,
安歇前有长长的路要走。

Dust of Snow

The way a crow

Shook down on me

The dust of snow

From a hemlock tree

Has given my heart

A change of mood

And saved some part

Of a day I had rued

雪 尘

一只乌鸦
朝我俯冲的样子
宛如雪尘
从铁杉抖落的样子

这让我的颓废
有了些微起色
也让我一天的懊悔
得到了部分救赎

The Pasture

I'm going out to clean the pasture spring;
I'll only stop to rake the leaves away
(And wait to watch the water clear, I may):
I shan't be gone long.—You come too.

I'm going out to fetch the little calf
That's standing by the mother. It's so young,
It totters when she licks it with her tongue.
I shan't be gone long.—You come too.

牧　场

我要出门清理牧场的泉水；
只需停下来把叶子耙成一堆
（我可以静静等待，看水变清浅）：
我不会久留。——你不妨也来。

我要出门牵回外面的小牛
它站在母牛身边，如此稚嫩，
当被妈妈舔舐的时候，它站立不稳。
我不会久待。——你不妨也来。

Thomas Hardy

[英国] 托马斯·哈代

1840—1928

哈代是英国文学史上最负盛名的诗人和小说家之一,他的写作生涯横跨了维多利亚时代和现代。他优美的抒情诗影响了弗罗斯特、奥登、拉金等诗人,其作品与生活息息相关,现代色彩浓厚。

The Fallow Deer At the Lonely House

One without looks in to-night

Through the curtain-chink

From the sheet of glistening white;

One without looks in to-night

As we sit and think

By the fender-brink.

We do not discern those eyes

Watching in the snow;

Lit by lamps of rosy dyes

We do not discern those eyes

Wondering, aglow,

Fourfooted, tiptoe.

孤宅前的麋鹿

今晚无人向屋内张望
透过窗帘的缝隙
站在窗外,地面泛着白莹莹的光;
今晚无人向屋内张望
我们坐在壁炉的栅栏边
不由自主地想。

我们没发现那双眼睛
正在雪地里朝此处观望;
粉色的灯光晃着视线
我们没发现那双眼睛
出着神,映着光,
踮着脚尖,四蹄轻扬。

The Caged Thrush Freed and Home Again (Villanelle)

"Men know but little more than we,
Who count us least of things terrene,
How happy days are made to be!

"Of such strange tidings what think ye,
O birds in brown that peck and preen?
Men know but little more than we!

"When I was borne from yonder tree
In bonds to them, I hoped to glean
How happy days are made to be,

"And want and wailing turned to glee;
Alas, despite their mighty mien
Men know but little more than we!

"They cannot change the Frost's decree,
They cannot keep the skies serene;

How happy days are made to be

Eludes great Man's sagacity
No less than ours, O tribes in treen!
Men know but little more than we
How happy days are made to be."

笼中的画眉获释返家（维拉内拉）

"人类把我们视为地球上最渺小的生物，
他们懂的却不比我们多，
多么自以为是的快活日子呵！

"哦，终日啄食和理毛的棕色小鸟，
对于如此奇怪的消息你怎么看？
人类懂的不比我们多！

"我在那边的树上被人类捕获
在与他们的交往中，我希望收集证据
多么自以为是的快活日子呵，

"匮乏和哀鸣化为了幸灾乐祸；
啊，尽管他们外表强悍
人类懂的不比我们多！

"他们无法更改严寒的律令，
他们无法保持天空的平静；
多么自以为是的快活日子呵

"撇开伟人的智慧不谈

那不亚于我们的智慧。哦,树上的部落!

人类懂的不比我们多!

多么自以为是的快活日子呵。"

To Flowers From Italy in Winter

Sunned in the South, and here to-day;
—If all organic things
Be sentient, Flowers, as some men say,
What are your ponderings?

How can you stay, nor vanish quite
From this bleak spot of thorn,
And birch, and fir, and frozen white
Expanse of the forlorn?

Frail luckless exiles hither brought!
Your dust will not regain
Old sunny haunts of Classic thought
When you shall waste and wane;

But mix with alien earth, be lit
With frigid Boreal flame,
And not a sign remain in it
To tell men whence you came.

致严冬里的意大利花儿

你本该在南方沐浴阳光,如今却沦落到这儿;
如果像一些人说的那样
一切有机物都有感觉,包括花儿,
那你的感觉又怎样?

你是怎样坚守下来,而没有
从这荒凉的荆棘之地消失?
在这广袤的荒芜之处,
白桦、冷杉和冰天雪地就是所有。

孱弱不幸的流亡者被带来了!
你的尘埃不会再回来
你的躯体日渐衰朽了
阳光般温暖的记忆不会再回来;

但与异域的土地产生交集,
你被寒冷的北方火焰点亮,
没有一丝痕迹留存
告诉人们你曾来自何方。

Song of Hope

O sweet To-morrow!—

After to-day

There will away

This sense of sorrow.

Then let us borrow

Hope, for a gleaming

Soon will be streaming,

Dimmed by no gray—

No gray!

While the winds wing us

Sighs from The Gone,

Nearer to dawn

Minute-beats bring us;

When there will sing us

Larks of a glory

Waiting our story

Further anon—

Anon!

Doff the black token,

Don the red shoon,

Right and retune

Viol-strings broken;

Null the words spoken

In speeches of rueing,

The night cloud is hueing,

To-morrow shines soon—

Shines soon!

希望之歌

哦,甜蜜的明天!
过了今日,
这惆怅的情感
就会消逝。
然后,让我们借来
希望,因为希望之光
很快就会流淌,
不再有晦暗,
没有晦暗!

当风的翅膀吹送着我们
对昨日的叹息,
就要在黎明止息,
每分每秒的跳动都带给我们;
云雀的歌声送给我们
辉煌与荣耀,
等候我们的捷报。
就快来了,
快来了!

摘掉黑色的标记，

穿上红色的鞋子，

重新调整步子，

中提琴的低音戛然而止；

让颓丧的陈词中，

所有抱怨的话终止。

夜色里的云正在苏醒，

明早的太阳即将照射四方，

将照射四方！

John Keats

[英国] 约翰·济慈

1795—1821

英国诗人济慈是浪漫主义诗歌的先驱。他的诗作无论从形式还是内容上,都体现了对美的极致追求,对后世影响深远。

Ode on a Grecian Urn

Thou still unravish'd bride of quietness,
Thou foster-child of silence and slow time,
Sylvan historian, who canst thus express
A flowery tale more sweetly than our rhyme:
What leaf-fring'd legend haunts about thy shape
Of deities or mortals, or of both,
In Tempe or the dales of Arcady?
What men or gods are these? What maidens loth?
What mad pursuit? What struggle to escape?
What pipes and timbrels? What wild ecstasy?

Heard melodies are sweet, but those unheard
Are sweeter; therefore, ye soft pipes, play on;
Not to the sensual ear, but, more endear'd,
Pipe to the spirit ditties of no tone:
Fair youth, beneath the trees, thou canst not leave
Thy song, nor ever can those trees be bare;
Bold Lover, never, never canst thou kiss,
Though winning near the goal yet, do not grieve;

She cannot fade, though thou hast not thy bliss,

For ever wilt thou love, and she be fair!

Ah, happy, happy boughs! that cannot shed

Your leaves, nor ever bid the Spring adieu;

And, happy melodist, unwearied,

For ever piping songs for ever new;

More happy love! more happy, happy love!

For ever warm and still to be enjoy'd,

For ever panting, and for ever young;

All breathing human passion far above,

That leaves a heart high-sorrowful and cloy'd,

A burning forehead, and a parching tongue.

Who are these coming to the sacrifice?

To what green altar, O mysterious priest,

Lead'st thou that heifer lowing at the skies,

And all her silken flanks with garlands drest?

What little town by river or sea shore,

Or mountain-built with peaceful citadel,

Is emptied of this folk, this pious morn?

And, little town, thy streets for evermore
Will silent be; and not a soul to tell
Why thou art desolate, can e'er return.

O Attic shape! Fair attitude! with brede
Of marble men and maidens overwrought,
With forest branches and the trodden weed;
Thou, silent form, dost tease us out of thought
As doth eternity: Cold Pastoral!
When old age shall this generation waste,
Thou shalt remain, in midst of other woe
Than ours, a friend to man, to whom thou say'st,
"Beauty is truth, truth beauty,—that is all
Ye know on earth, and all ye need to know."

希腊古瓮颂

你是安宁的新娘,依然童贞未失,
你的父母是寂静无声和悠长时光,
山林中的史学家,你能够绘制
如花的故事,比我们的诗篇还辉煌:
你身旁萦绕着以绿叶镶边的传说
关于神仙还是凡人,亦或二者兼有?
在坦佩的溪谷还是阿卡狄的山谷?
他们是何方神圣?竟让少女如此为难?
多么疯狂的追求?怎样挣扎着逃走?
什么笛子和手鼓?多么狂野的喜悦?

入耳的旋律美妙,然而那未听见的
更加甜蜜;所以,婉转的风笛请继续演奏;
不是为了愉悦耳朵,而是要变得
更为迷人,为灵魂吹出无声的节奏:
树荫下的美少年,你不能抛下
你的歌,就像树木也不能丢下绿叶;
冲动的求爱者,你永远也吻她不到,
虽然无比接近目标。但,不要哀叹;

她永远不会消失,尽管你爱而不得,
你将求爱不止,她将容颜不老!

啊,欢欣鼓舞的枝条!你不会
抖落绿叶,也不会和春天惜别;
还有快乐的作曲家,永不疲惫
一直在更新,一直在吹奏;
更多欢畅的爱!无尽欢畅的爱!
永远热流涌动,仍堪被人享用,
永远执着渴望,永远青春萌动;
它超越所有不死的人间欲望,
那欲望让人前额滚烫、口干舌燥,
还使人悲痛难耐、心神烦忧。

前来献祭的是何许人也?
要去哪座绿色的祭坛?哦,神秘的祭司,
你领着那头仰天长啸的母牛,
顺滑的腰间缀满美丽的花环。
要去哪座河畔小镇或海港小城?
或是依山而建的宁静城堡?
在这祭神的清晨,是否万人空巷?

小镇呵,你的街道永远缄默,

若有人讲述你寂寞的原因,

他就永远无法故地重返。

噢,雅典的形体!气质的绝妙!

大理石的饰带,缠绕众人身上,

还有森林的枝条,踩过的野草;

你以沉默的姿态,引领我们超越尘想

如同亘古一样:冷峻的田园牧歌!

当这一代人的韶华逝去,

你将超越世俗的悲伤,你仍然是

人类的朋友,对着他们如此布道:

"美即是真,真即是美。这就是

你们在人间了解的一切,也是你们需要知道的一切。"

Stanzas

In drear-nighted December,

Too happy, happy tree,

Thy branches ne'er remember

Their green felicity:

The north cannot undo them

With a sleety whistle through them;

Nor frozen thawings glue them

From budding at the prime.

In drear-nighted December,

Too happy, happy brook,

Thy bubblings ne'er remember

Apollo's summer look;

But with a sweet forgetting,

They stay their crystal fretting,

Never, never petting

About the frozen time.

Ah! would 'twere so with many

A gentle girl and boy!
But were there ever any
Writhed not at passed joy?
The feel of not to feel it,
When there is none to heal it,
Nor numbed sense to steel it,
Was never said in rhyme.

诗 节

在夜色阴冷的十二月，
多么快乐、快乐的小树，
你的枝条从不记得
它们曾林阴如瀑：
北风也拿它们无可奈何，
即使雨雪呼啸而过；
将融的冰雪也凝固不了
它们在春天萌发的新苗。

在夜色阴冷的十二月，
多么快乐、快乐的小溪，
你的泡沫从不记得
阿波罗盛夏的生机：
但带着甜蜜的遗忘，
它们保持着水晶般的微荡，
从不、从不郁结
冰天雪地的时节。

啊！但愿少男少女

也和你们一样安之若素!
然而世间是否有人
不为逝去的快乐而痛苦?
无法保持麻木,
明知于事无补,
也不能用迟钝去抵御,
这无奈在诗歌里尚无人诉苦。

To My Brothers

Small, busy flames play through the fresh-laid coals,
And their faint cracklings o'er our silence creep
Like whispers of the household gods that keep
A gentle empire o'er fraternal souls.
And while for rhymes I search around the poles,
Your eyes are fixed, as in poetic sleep,
Upon the lore so voluble and deep,
That aye at fall of night our care condoles.
This is your birthday, Tom, and I rejoice
That thus it passes smoothly, quietly:
Many such eves of gently whispering noise
May we together pass, and calmly try
What are this world's true joys,—ere the great Voice
From its fair face shall bid our spirits fly.

致我的兄弟们

小小的、顽皮的火苗在新添的煤上跳跃，

它们微弱的噼啪声映衬着我们的沉默，

蹑手蹑脚如家神的低声啰嗦，

像一个温和的帝国映衬着兄弟的魂魄。

为赋新词，我绕着柱子苦苦思索，

你目不转睛，仿佛在诗的梦境徜徉，

这段传说，如此跌宕绵长，

那个秋天的夜晚，我们相互抚慰忧伤。

今天是你的生日，汤姆，我为你感到欣慰

因为时光在安静地流淌。

许多个这样温柔低语的夜晚，

愿我们一起度过，沉静地体味

这世上真正的欢愉，——当神的声音

从他公正的脸庞发出，我们的灵魂将展翅飞翔。

A Thing of Beauty (Endymion)

A thing of beauty is a joy for ever:
Its lovliness increases; it will never
Pass into nothingness; but still will keep
A bower quiet for us, and a sleep
Full of sweet dreams, and health, and quiet breathing.
Therefore, on every morrow, are we wreathing
A flowery band to bind us to the earth,
Spite of despondence, of the inhuman dearth
Of noble natures, of the gloomy days,
Of all the unhealthy and o'er-darkn'd ways
Made for our searching: yes, in spite of all,
Some shape of beauty moves away the pall
From our dark spirits. Such the sun, the moon,
Trees old and young, sprouting a shady boon
For simple sheep; and such are daffodils
With the green world they live in; and clear rills
That for themselves a cooling covert make
'Gainst the hot season; the mid-forest brake,

Rich with a sprinkling of fair musk-rose blooms:

And such too is the grandeur of the dooms

We have imagined for the mighty dead;

An endless fountain of immortal drink,

Pouring unto us from the heaven's brink.

美的事物（恩底弥翁）

美的事物是永恒的抚慰：

它的美好与日俱增，从来不会

堕入虚无；它为我们保全

一片静谧的树阴；让睡眠

充满甜梦、健康和安详的呼吸。

因此，在每个明天，让我们编织

一个花环，把我们与泥土结合在一起，

尽管时有沮丧，尽管人类高贵的品性

常常缺席，尽管时有愁云惨雾，

尽管卑劣、阴暗的小路就在沿途

供我们寻找：是的，尽管这些让人哀叹，

但总有某种形式的美吹散

我们幽暗心灵的迷雾。比如太阳、月亮，

比如老树和新株，为无忧无虑的羊

萌发一片阴凉；还有水仙

和它们生活的绿色家园；还有清澈的溪流

为它们自己打造凉爽的矮树丛，

以此抵御烈日炎炎；再如林间的灌木丛，

星星点点洒满了麝香蔷薇的美丽花瓣：

还有我们为逝去的伟人做出的评判,

那是想象中的结局的完满;

这是一汪长生不老的无尽甘泉,

从天边注入我们的心田。

注:恩底弥翁(Endymion),希腊神话中的美男子。

D. H. Lawrence
[英国]戴维·赫伯特·劳伦斯
1885—1930

劳伦斯是19世纪的英国小说家、诗人,曾因为《查特莱夫人的情人》一书而饱受争议。作为诗人,他是位不折不扣的浪漫主义者,信奉爱情至上。他反对工业文明,钟情大自然和植物,写下了许多真诚又动人的诗篇。

Dream-Confused

Is that the moon

At the window so big and red?

No one in the room,

No one near the bed—?

Listen, her shoon

Palpitating down the stair?

—Or a beat of wings at the window there?

A moment ago

She kissed me warm on the mouth,

The very moon in the south

Is warm with a bloody glow,

The moon from far abysses

Signalling those two kisses.

And now the moon

Goes slowly out of the west,

And slowly back in my breast

My kisses are sinking, soon

To leave me at rest.

迷乱的梦

那是一轮月亮么,
在窗边巨大猩红的那个东西?
无人在房间里,
也无人在床边?

听,是不是她脚上的鞋子
正飞快地跳下楼梯?
还是一双翅膀在窗边拍打的声音?

就在刚才
她在我唇边留下一个温暖的吻,
南边的那个月亮
同样温暖地闪着血光,
月亮从遥远的深渊赶来
暗示了刚才的两个吻。

此刻这轮月亮
缓缓地从西边消失了,
缓缓地回到我的胸口

我的吻在沉降,很快
就会放我进入梦乡。

A White Blossom

A tiny moon as white and small as a single jasmine flower
Leans all alone above my window, on night's wintry bower,
Liquid as lime-tree blossom, soft as brilliant water or rain
She shines, the one white love of my youth, which all sin cannot stain.

一朵白色的花

月亮皎洁娇小,像一朵兀自开放的茉莉。
她孤单单倚在我的窗口,在夜晚的冬日凉亭里,
如菩提花朵一般多汁,又如甘泉雨水一样柔软。
月色如银,那是我青春的纯白之恋,没有罪孽能将它污染。

Bei Hennef

The little river twittering in the twilight,
The wan, wondering look of the pale sky,
This is almost bliss.

And everything shut up and gone to sleep,
All the troubles and anxieties and pain
Gone under the twilight.

Only the twilight now, and the soft "Sh!" of the river
That will last for ever.

And at last I know my love for you is here,
I can see it all, it is whole like the twilight,
It is large, so large, I could not see it before
Because of the little lights and flickers and interruptions,
Troubles, anxieties and pains.

You are the call and I am the answer,
You are the wish, and I the fulfilment,

You are the night, and I the day.

What else—it is perfect enough,

It is perfectly complete,

You and I,

What more—?

Strange, how we suffer in spite of this!

在汉尼夫近郊

小河在暮色里闪着微光,
苍白天空露出娇弱又探询的模样,
这几乎是一段极乐时光。

万物都熄灭熟睡,
世间的烦恼、焦虑和心碎
在暮色里悄然退场。

此刻只有霭霭暮色,和河流
那无休无止的"嘘"声温柔。

我终于明了对你的爱就在此地,
我遍览它的一切,爱像暮色一样完整,
它广袤无边,此前我却不曾看见。
都怪那闪烁的微光和间或的搅扰,
都怨那烦恼、焦虑和心碎。

你是呼喊,我就是回应,
你是许愿,我就是显灵,

你是夜晚，我就是白昼。

还缺什么——已经足够，

已经足够完整，

你我之间，

还缺什么？

吊诡的是，即便如此，活着依旧让人难受！

Green

The dawn was apple-green,

The sky was green wine held up in the sun,

The moon was a golden petal between.

She opened her eyes, and green

They shone, clear like flowers undone

For the first time, now for the first time seen.

绿

黎明是一抹苹果绿,

天空是骄阳下举起的碧绿美酒,

月亮是美酒里漂浮的一片金色花瓣。

她睁开她的眼睛,我看到了绿,

眼波流转,像含苞待放的花儿一样清澈。

这是人生中的第一次,它们第一次被看见。

Butterfly

Butterfly, the wind blows sea-ward,
strong beyond the garden-wall!
Butterfly, why do you settle on my
shoe, and sip the dirt on my shoe,
Lifting your veined wings, lifting them?
big white butterfly!

Already it is October, and the wind
blows strong to the sea
from the hills where snow must have
fallen, the wind is polished with
snow.
Here in the garden, with red
geraniums, it is warm, it is warm
but the wind blows strong to sea-ward,
white butterfly, content on my shoe!

Will you go, will you go from my warm
house?

Will you climb on your big soft wings,
black-dotted,
as up an invisible rainbow, an arch
till the wind slides you sheer from the arch-crest
and in a strange level fluttering you go
out to sea-ward, white speck!

蝴　蝶

蝴蝶，风吹向大海，
狂风一直吹过花园的围墙！
蝴蝶，你为何停在我的鞋子上，
还在我的鞋子上啜饮泥土，
扬起你的脉翅，扬起它们？
大大的白色蝴蝶！

已经是十月了，狂风
吹向大海，
从注定落满了白雪的山丘吹过，
连风也被雪花装点。
这里的花园开满红色的天竺葵，很暖很暖。
但是狂风一直吹向大海，
白色的蝴蝶，为能栖息在我的鞋子上而满足！

你会离开么？你会从我温暖的家园
离开么？
你会爬上你硕大柔软的翅膀么？
那双布满黑色斑点的翅膀，

就像爬上一弯看不见的拱形彩虹,

直到风使你从拱顶滑落。

你以奇特的角度振颤着翅膀

飞向大海,最后化为小小的白点!

Amy Lowell

[美国]艾米·洛威尔

1874—1925

艾米·洛威尔是位个性十足的美国女诗人、演员、编辑、译者。她喜欢穿男装,抽雪茄。她热爱中国古典诗歌,是意象派运动的领袖之一。她曾说:"上帝把我造就成一个商人,可我让自己成了诗人。"

At Night

The wind is singing through the trees to-night,
A deep-voiced song of rushing cadences
And crashing intervals. No summer breeze
Is this, though hot July is at its height,
Gone is her gentler music; with delight
She listens to this booming like the seas,
These elemental, loud necessities
Which call to her to answer their swift might.
Above the tossing trees shines down a star,
Quietly bright; this wild, tumultuous joy
Quickens nor dims its splendour. And my mind,
O Star! is filled with your white light, from far,
So suffer me this one night to enjoy
The freedom of the onward sweeping wind.

在夜晚

今晚风在树林中吟唱,

一首深沉的歌曲,伴随着急促的节奏

和激烈的音程。这绝非

夏日的微风,尽管炎热的七月正值高峰。

她温柔的音乐已经飘散,愉快地

聆听这如大海般的轰鸣,

这些原始、高亢的必然轰鸣

呼唤她回应它们迅疾的力量。

随风摇摆的树林上空,一颗星星洒下光辉,

静静地明亮着;这种狂野、喧闹的欢乐

不增也不减它的光芒。还有我的心,

远方的星星啊!我的心盈满了你皎洁的光,

所以这一晚就让我痛并享受着

自由的风吹过。

Sea Shell

Sea Shell, Sea Shell,
Sing me a song, O Please!
A song of ships, and sailor men,
And parrots, and tropical trees,
Of islands lost in the Spanish Main
Which no man ever may find again,
Of fishes and corals under the waves,
And seahorses stabled in great green caves.
Sea Shell, Sea Shell,
Sing of the things you know so well.

贝　壳

贝壳，贝壳

请为我唱一首歌！

一首关于轮船和水手的歌，

还有鹦鹉，还有热带丛林，

歌唱西班牙大陆失落的岛屿，

人们再也寻觅不见的故土，

一首关于浪花下鱼儿和珊瑚的歌，

还有碧绿洞穴里一动不动的海马。

贝壳，贝壳，

歌唱你所熟悉的一切吧。

Dreams

I do not care to talk to you although

Your speech evokes a thousand sympathies,

And all my being's silent harmonies

Wake trembling into music. When you go

It is as if some sudden, dreadful blow

Had severed all the strings with savage ease.

No, do not talk; but let us rather seize

This intimate gift of silence which we know.

Others may guess your thoughts from what you say,

As storms are guessed from clouds where darkness broods.

To me the very essence of the day

Reveals its inner purpose and its moods;

As poplars feel the rain and then straightway

Reverse their leaves and shimmer through the woods.

梦

我不想和你说话,尽管
你的言语唤起无数共鸣,
而我所有沉默的和声都
在颤抖的音乐中苏醒。当你走的时候,
仿佛某次突然又致命的一击,
以蛮力使所有的琴弦轻易断裂。
不,不要说话;倒不如让我们抓住
我们所熟悉的这种叫作沉默的亲密礼物。
其他人可能依托你的言语猜出你的想法,
如同从乌云笼罩中猜出暴风雨的来临一样。
对我来说,一天的本质
揭示了它内在的目的和情绪;
就像白杨感受到了雨水,而后立刻
翻转它们的叶子,在树林间熠熠发光。

To A Friend

I ask but one thing of you, only one,

That always you will be my dream of you;

That never shall I wake to find untrue

All this I have believed and rested on,

Forever vanished, like a vision gone

Out into the night. Alas, how few

There are who strike in us a chord we knew

Existed, but so seldom heard its tone

We tremble at the half-forgotten sound.

The world is full of rude awakenings

And heaven-born castles shattered to the ground,

Yet still our human longing vainly clings

To a belief in beauty through all wrongs.

O stay your hand, and leave my heart its songs!

致一位友人

我对你只有一事相求,只有一件,
就是你要一直和我梦中的你相同;
我永远不必在梦醒后发现
我信仰与依赖的一切,
就此无影无踪,仿佛幻象
消失在夜空中。唉,默契多么罕见。
我们清楚彼此间的共鸣
的确存在,但很少听到它的琴弦。
我们只能对着半被忘却的音乐颤抖。
这世间充满了粗暴的打断,
天堂里铸就的城堡终将塌陷,
然而我们的人性执着于徒劳的信仰,
穿越所有的谬误,抓住美好不放。
哦,不要松开你的手,让我的心还能歌唱!

The Crescent Moon

Slipping softly through the sky
Little horned, happy moon,
Can you hear me up so high?
Will you come down soon?
On my nursery window-sill
Will you stay your steady flight?
And then float away with me
Through the summer night?
Brushing over tops of trees,
Playing hide and seek with stars,
Peeping up through shiny clouds
At Jupiter or Mars.
I shall fill my lap with roses
Gathered in the milky way,
All to carry home to mother.
Oh! what will she say!
Little rocking, sailing moon,
Do you hear me shout — Ahoy!
Just a little nearer, moon,
To please a little boy.

新　月

轻轻地滑过天空
长着小小犄角的快乐月亮,
你在高高的天上能听到我吗?
你要不要快快下来?
落在我儿童房的窗台上
你能保持稳稳的飞行吗?
能带我一起飞翔
飞过夏日的夜空吗?
掠过大片的树冠,
和星星们玩捉迷藏,
透过闪亮的云层偷看
木星或者火星。
我要在我的双膝铺满
从银河采来的玫瑰,
把它们全带回家给妈妈。
哦!她会说什么?
摇摇摆摆、正在航海的小小月亮,
你听到我的叫声了吗——啊呵!
再离我近一些,月亮,
好让一个小小的男孩开心。

Claude McKay

[美国]克劳德·麦凯

1889—1948

克劳德·麦凯是一位非裔美国诗人,被称为"牙买加的彭斯"。他的诗歌清新优美,朗朗上口,对自然风光和生活片段进行了栩栩如生的刻画。

After the Winter

Some day, when trees have shed their leaves

And against the morning's white

The shivering birds beneath the eaves

Have sheltered for the night,

We'll turn our faces southward, love,

Toward the summer isle

Where bamboos spire the shafted grove

And wide-mouthed orchids smile.

And we will seek the quiet hill

Where towers the cotton tree,

And leaps the laughing crystal rill,

And works the droning bee.

And we will build a cottage there

Beside an open glade,

With black-ribbed blue-bells blowing near,

And ferns that never fade.

冬季过后

某天，待树木抖落叶片

迎来东方既白，

待屋檐下颤抖的鸟儿

熬过无边黑夜，

亲爱的，我们将面朝南方，

朝向夏日的岛屿。

那里的翠竹正破土而出，

那里的兰花正肆意绽放。

我们会寻到一处幽静的山丘，

比木棉树还高耸的地方，

那里的溪流欢腾奔涌，

那里的蜜蜂嗡嗡不休。

我们要在那里盖一座小屋，

就在林中的空地旁，

那里有黑色斑纹的蓝铃花随风摇曳，

那里还有蕨类植物永不凋谢。

Romance

To clasp you now and feel your head close-pressed,
Scented and warm against my beating breast;

To whisper soft and quivering your name,
And drink the passion burning in your frame;

To lie at full length, taut, with cheek to cheek,
And tease your mouth with kisses till you speak;

Love words, mad words, dream words, sweet senseless words,
Melodious like notes of mating birds;

To hear you ask if I shall love always,
And myself answer: Till the end of days;

To feel your easeful sigh of happiness
When on your trembling lips I murmur: Yes;

It is so sweet. We know it is not true.

What matters it? The night must shed her dew.

We know it is not true, but it is sweet—

The poem with this music is complete.

浪 漫

此刻抱紧你,感受你的头就贴在我的胸膛,
芬芳温暖,靠着我跳动的心脏;

温柔低语,轻声呼唤的是你的名字,
一饮而尽,尽情燃烧的是你的身子;

我们平躺,交织,脸颊对着脸颊,
用亲吻挑逗你的嘴唇,直到你开口说话;

情话、疯话、梦话,和傻傻的甜言蜜语,
像鸟儿求偶的歌声一样富有旋律;

听到你问我的爱是否会永不改变,
我的回答是:直到生命终止的那天;

我对着你颤抖的双唇柔声许诺,
感受你快乐又宽慰的叹息拂过;

爱的游戏如此甜蜜。我们清楚这未必真实。

但那又如何？洒下甘露就是夜晚的意义。

我们知道这未必真实，但爱的游戏如此甜蜜——
这首被谱曲的诗歌也因此书写完毕。

To One Coming North

At first you'll joy to see the playful snow,
Like white moths trembling on the tropic air,
Or waters of the hills that softly flow
Gracefully falling down a shining stair.

And when the fields and streets are covered white
And the wind-worried void is chilly, raw,
Or underneath a spell of heat and light
The cheerless frozen spots begin to thaw,

Like me you'll long for home, where birds' glad song
Means flowering lanes and leas and spaces dry,
And tender thoughts and feelings fine and strong,
Beneath a vivid silver-flecked blue sky.

But oh! more than the changeless southern isles,
When Spring has shed upon the earth her charm,
You'll love the Northland wreathed in golden smiles
By the miraculous sun turned glad and warm.

致来到北方的人

起初你会开心地看到顽皮的雪花,

宛如白色的飞蛾在热带的空中颤抖,

又像山里的清泉轻柔地流淌,

从闪亮的楼梯上优雅地落下。

当田野和街道都披上了白袍,

当狂风肆虐的天空阴冷又萧条,

热浪和阳光念起了咒语,

冰封的冻土开始融化,

你会像我一样渴望家乡,那里鸟儿终年鸣唱,

没有潮湿,无论花径、草地或是其他地方,

站在银色斑点的朗朗晴空下,

感觉自己温柔又坚强。

但是,哦!比起四季如春的南方群岛,

当春天对世界施展她的魅力,

你会爱上挂着金色笑容的北方大地,

那是太阳化冰冷为明快的奇迹。

I Shall Return

I shall return again; I shall return

To laugh and love and watch with wonder-eyes

At golden noon the forest fires burn,

Wafting their blue-black smoke to sapphire skies.

I shall return to loiter by the streams

That bathe the brown blades of the bending grasses,

And realize once more my thousand dreams

Of waters rushing down the mountain passes.

I shall return to hear the fiddle and fife

Of village dances, dear delicious tunes

That stir the hidden depths of native life,

Stray melodies of dim remembered runes.

I shall return, I shall return again,

To ease my mind of long, long years of pain.

我会回来

我会再次回到这里,我会回来。

笑着,爱着,用惊奇的眼神看着。

森林的火焰在金色的正午灼烧,

蓝黑色的烟雾向蓝宝石的天空飘着。

我会回到溪边闲荡,

草儿在风中摇晃,褐色的叶片被溪水浸润着,

我会把我的一千个梦重温,

梦见从山涧奔流而下的瀑布,汩汩流淌着。

我会回来听小提琴和横笛的音乐再次响起,

伴着乡村的舞蹈,美妙的曲调,

我会把深埋的乡愁再次唤起,

用走音的旋律书写着依稀记得的符号。

我会回来,我会再次回到这里,

抚慰自己多年的心伤和长久的惆怅。

Courage

O lonely heart so timid of approach,
Like the shy tropic flower that shuts its lips
To the faint touch of tender finger tips:
What is your word? What question would you broach?

Your lustrous-warm eyes are too sadly kind
To mask the meaning of your dreamy tale,
Your guarded life too exquisitely frail
Against the daggers of my warring mind.

There is no part of the unyielding earth,
Even bare rocks where the eagles build their nest,
Will give us undisturbed and friendly rest.
No dewfall softens this vast belt of dearth.

But in the socket-chiseled teeth of strife,
That gleam in serried files in all the lands,
We may join hungry, understanding hands,
And drink our share of ardent love and life.

勇 气

哦,孤独的心儿如此害怕被靠近,
就像娇羞的热带花朵闭上它的嘴唇。
温柔的指尖对着它轻轻一碰:
你想说什么?你要发出什么疑问?

你温暖明亮的双眸太过纯净,
掩饰不了你梦中呓语的浓情,
你那被呵护的生命太过娇弱,
对抗不了我思想的锋芒。

没有一块坚如磐石的土地,
可以让我们安心放松地休憩。
没有露水能滋润这大片的干涸,
即使老鹰筑巢的裸岩也不可以。

但在唇齿开合的嘈嘈挣扎中,
在所有疆土的凛凛寒光里,
我们可以紧握彼此饥渴默契的手,
痛饮这份热烈的爱情与活力。

Rabindranath Tagore

[印度]罗宾德拉纳特·泰戈尔

1861—1941

印度诗人、作家泰戈尔出生于一个艺术气氛浓厚的贵族家庭,少年时代就开始写诗。泰戈尔的写作生涯超过六十年,在文学和艺术上取得了巨大的成就。他以赞美诗《吉檀迦利》成为第一位获得诺贝尔文学奖的亚洲人。

Gitanjali 35

Where the mind is without fear and the head is held high;
Where knowledge is free;
Where the world has not been broken up into fragments by narrow domestic walls;
Where words come out from the depth of truth;
Where tireless striving stretches its arms towards perfection;
Where the clear stream of reason has not lost its way into the dreary desert sand of dead habit;
Where the mind is led forward by thee into ever-widening thought and action
Into that heaven of freedom, my Father, let my country awake.

《吉檀迦利》第35首

在那里,心中无所畏惧,头颅高高扬起;

在那里,知识即自由;

在那里,世界没有因为封闭的高墙而支离破碎;

在那里,语言源自真理的深处;

在那里,不倦的奋斗向完美伸出双臂;

在那里,理性的清泉还没有迷失在积习的荒漠;

在那里,头脑在你的引领下走向越发开阔的思想和行动,

进入自由的殿堂,我的天父啊,让我的祖国觉醒吧。

Keep me fully glad...II

Keep me fully glad with nothing. Only take my hand in your hand.
In the gloom of the deepening night take up my heart and play with it as you list. Bind me close to you with nothing.
I will spread myself out at your feet and lie still. Under this clouded sky I will meet silence with silence. I will become one with the night clasping the earth in my breast.
Make my life glad with nothing.
The rains sweep the sky from end to end. Jasmines in the wet untamable wind revel in their own perfume. The cloud-hidden stars thrill in secret. Let me fill to the full my heart with nothing but my own depth of joy.

让我满心欢喜……2

你一无所有,就让我满心欢喜。你只需把我的手放在你的手心。

在午夜的阴霾中捧起我的心,如你所愿,随意把玩。

你一无所有,就紧紧地将我和你绑在一起。

我会在你的脚边舒展开来,一动不动。在这片多云的天空下我将以沉默对峙沉默。在我的胸中,夜晚拥抱着大地,我终于完整。

你一无所有,就让我满心欢喜。

雨水从头到尾扫过天空。茉莉在潮湿的狂风中陶醉于自己的香气。躲在阴云背后的星星正偷偷地欢庆。让我一无所有,只用深深的欢喜,就把自己的心填满。

The Gardener 85

Who are you, reader, reading my poems an hundred years hence?
I cannot send you one single flower from this wealth of the spring, one single streak of gold from yonder clouds.
Open your doors and look abroad.

From your blossoming garden gather fragrant memories of the vanished flowers of an hundred years before.
In the joy of your heart may you feel the living joy that sang one spring morning, sending its glad voice across an hundred years.

《园丁集》第 85 首

你是谁,这位读者,在百年之后读着我的诗歌?
在春天的盛宴里,我连一枝鲜花也无法赠你,在遥远的彩云里,我连一缕金色也无法送你。
打开你的门,向外眺望吧。

从你繁茂的花园里收集芬芳的记忆,那是百年之前消逝的花儿留下的记忆。
在你满心的喜悦中,愿你从歌声里感受春天的早晨那生机勃勃的欢乐,并让它欢乐的声音一直飘散到百年之后。

Playthings

Child, how happy you are sitting in the dust, playing with a broken twig all the morning.
I smile at your play with that little bit of a broken twig.
I am busy with my accounts, adding up figures by the hour.
Perhaps you glance at me and think, "What a stupid game to spoil your morning with!"
Child, I have forgotten the art of being absorbed in sticks and mud-pies.
I seek out costly playthings, and gather lumps of gold and silver.
With whatever you find you create your glad games, I spend both my time and my strength over things I never can obtain.
In my frail canoe I struggle to cross the sea of desire, and forget that I too am playing a game.

玩 具

孩子，你是多么快乐，整个上午都坐在泥土里，玩着一根折断的树枝。

我微笑着看你摆弄那一小截断裂的树枝。

时间分分秒秒地过去了，我正忙着算账，把数字们叠加起来。

也许你扫了我一眼，暗自想："多么愚蠢的游戏啊，毁了你的一整个上午！"

孩子，我已经忘记了沉浸于木棍和泥巴的艺术。

我寻求昂贵的玩具，收集大块的金银之物。

无论你找到了什么，你总能创造出快乐的游戏，而我把时间和力气都放在了我永远得不到的东西上。

乘着我摇摇晃晃的独木舟，我挣扎着试图穿越欲望的海洋，却忘记了我不过也在做游戏而已。

Song VII (Sing the song of the moment...)

Sing the song of the moment in careless carols, in the transient light of the day;
Sing of the fleeting smiles that vanish and never look back;
Sing of the flowers that bloom and fade without regret.
Weave not in memory's thread the days that would glide into nights.
To the guests that must go bid God-speed, and wipe away all traces of their steps.
Let the moments end in moments with their cargo of fugitive songs.

With both hands snap the fetters you made with your own heart chords;
Take to your breast with a smile what is easy and simple and near.
Today is the festival of phantoms that know not when they die.
Let your laughter flush in meaningless mirth like

twinkles of light on the ripples;

Let your life lightly dance on the verge of Time like a dew on the tip of a leaf.

Strike in the chords of your harp the fitful murmurs of moments.

歌 7（唱此刻的歌……）

唱此刻的歌，在转瞬即逝的阳光下唱无心的颂歌；

唱灿烂而后褪色的笑容，那笑容不曾回首；

唱怒放而后凋谢的花朵，那花朵并无忧愁。

对那些将遁入黑夜的白昼，别把它们织入记忆的丝线。

对那些注定要告别的客人，祝他们一路顺风，并抹去他们的所有。

让此刻就结束在此刻，只吟唱短暂的歌。

用双手折断你以心弦铸就的藩篱；

用胸怀拥抱那些纯真无邪的微笑。

今天是魅影的节日，他们不知何时会离去。

让你的笑容如粼粼波光，除了快乐再无所图。

让你的生命在时间的边缘轻舞，仿佛叶尖的露珠。

让你竖琴的和弦弹奏出此刻的低语，若有似无。

Sara Teasdale

[美国]萨拉·提斯黛尔

1884—1933

萨拉·提斯黛尔是 20 世纪初美国的抒情诗人,普利策诗歌奖的首位获得者。在她崭露头角的年代,庞德和艾略特也没有她受欢迎。她是位细腻、孱弱的女诗人,擅长描写女性的情思,笔触华丽、凄美,让人动容。

Leaves

One by one, like leaves from a tree,

All my faiths have forsaken me;

But the stars above my head

Burn in white and delicate red,

And beneath my feet the earth

Brings the sturdy grass to birth.

I who was content to be

But a silken-singing tree,

But a rustle of delight

In the wistful heart of night,

I have lost the leaves that knew

Touch of rain and weight of dew.

Blinded by a leafy crown

I looked neither up nor down—

But the little leaves that die

Have left me room to see the sky;

Now for the first time I know

Stars above and earth below.

叶 子

像片片叶子从树上掉落，
我所有的信仰都已失落；
但当我仰望头顶的星光
五彩斑斓，群星闪亮，
当我俯瞰脚下的大地
枯又复荣，充满生机。
我曾满足于做一棵树，
浅吟低唱，如泣如诉，
在黯然心伤的每个晚上，
树叶沙沙，带来欢畅，
失去了那些叶子我便错过
雨水淅沥和露珠洒落。
我被浓密的树冠遮蔽
看不到天，见不到地——
然而那些掉落的叶片
让我得以抬头望天；
如今我才第一次熟悉
头顶的星光，脚下的大地。

The Answer

When I go back to earth
And all my joyous body
Puts off the red and white
That once had been so proud,
If men should pass above
With false and feeble pity,
My dust will find a voice
To answer them aloud:

"Be still, I am content,
Take back your poor compassion—
Joy was a flame in me
Too steady to destroy.
Lithe as a bending reed
Loving the storm that sways her—
I found more joy in sorrow
Than you could find in joy."

答 案

当我重返大地
带着我欢乐的身体
丢掉红色和白色
曾经如此骄傲的它们,
如果从头顶经过的路人
怀着些微虚伪的怜悯,
我会从尘土中发出声音
并大声地回答他们:

"安静些,我很知足,
请收回你们可怜的同情心——
我心中的幸福就像火焰,
太过炙热,难以扑灭。
如弯曲的簧片一般柔韧
她爱着撕扯她的风暴——
我在悲伤里找到的幸福
不比你在快乐里找到的少。"

Winter Stars

I went out at night alone,
The young blood flowing beyond the sea
Seemed to have drenched my spirit's wings—
I bore my sorrow heavily.

But when I lifted up my head
From shadows shaken on the snow,
I saw Orion in the east
Burn steadily as long ago.

From windows in my father's house,
Dreaming my dreams on winter nights,
I watched Orion as a girl
Above another city's lights.

Years go, dreams go, and youth goes too,
The world's heart breaks beneath its wars,
All things are changed, save in the east
The faithful beauty of the stars.

冬日的星

我独自一人在夜晚出门,
年轻的血液流过海洋
似乎浸透了我灵魂的翅膀——
我背负着沉甸甸的忧伤。

然而当我抬头仰望,
从雪地里晃动的影子上,
我看到了东方的猎户座
和亘古之前一样闪亮。

透过我父亲居所的窗户,
在冬日的夜晚梦着我的梦想,
孩提时的我便望着猎户座
高悬在另一座城的灯火之上。

年年岁岁,梦想逝去,韶华也逝去,
战火纷飞,世界已然心碎,
物是人非,唯有东方的星
容颜不改,美丽没有消退。

I Thought of You

I thought of you and how you love this beauty,
And walking up the long beach all alone
I heard the waves breaking in measured thunder
As you and I once heard their monotone.

Around me were the echoing dunes, beyond me
The cold and sparkling silver of the sea—
We two will pass through death and ages lengthen
Before you hear that sound again with me.

我想起了你

我想起了你,你是多么爱这美景,
孤独一人,沿着长长的沙滩漫步。
我听到浪花翻滚,就像雷声轰鸣,
如同你我,曾经听过的单调曲目。

沙丘的回声在周围起伏又穿越,
大海冰冷刺骨,银光闪闪——
我们将携手走过死亡和衰老,
在你我重温那涛声之前。

The Voice

Atoms as old as stars,
Mutation on mutation,
Millions and millions of cells
Dividing, yet still the same;
From air and changing earth,
From ancient Eastern rivers,
From turquoise tropic seas,
Unto myself I came.

My spirit like my flesh,
Sprang from a thousand sources,
From cave-man, hunter and shepherd,
From Karnak, Cyprus, Rome;
The living thoughts in me
Spring from dead men and women,
Forgotten time out of mind
And many as bubbles of foam.

Here for a moment's space

Into the light out of darkness,

I come and they come with me

Finding words with my breath;

From the wisdom of many life-times

I hear them cry: "Forever

Seek for Beauty, she only

Fights with man against Death."

声 音

繁星般古老的原子
突变接着突变,
数以百万的细胞
分离但依然相同,
空气和变迁的大地,
远古的东方河流,
绿松石色的热带海洋,
这就是我的来历。

我的精神如同我的肉体
从一千个源头迸发,
穴居人、猎人和牧羊人,
卡尔纳克、塞浦路斯和罗马;
我所有的灵感和想法
从死去的男女身上迸发,
时间已被忘却,
仿佛无数泡沫。

在这片刻的空间里

摆脱黑暗,进入光明,
我来了,他们也如影随形,
用呼吸寻找我的语言;
许多人用毕生的智慧
喊出如下的话语:"永远
追求美,只有她
与人类并肩对抗死神!"

Walt Whitman

[美国] 沃尔特·惠特曼

1819—1892

惠特曼是让美国人引以为傲的诗人,他与狄金森一起被称为美国现代派诗歌的先驱。他的《草叶集》讴歌了自然、爱情和友谊,歌颂人的身体和灵魂,对之后的现代派诗人产生了不可磨灭的影响。

On the Beach at Night Alone

On the beach at night alone,
As the old mother sways her to and fro singing her husky song,
As I watch the bright stars shining, I think a thought of the clef of the universes and of the future.

A vast similitude interlocks all,
All spheres, grown, ungrown, small, large, suns, moons, planets,
All distances of place however wide,
All distances of time, all inanimate forms,
All souls, all living bodies though they be ever so different, or in different worlds,
All gaseous, watery, vegetable, mineral processes, the fishes, the brutes,
All nations, colors, barbarisms, civilizations, languages,
All identities that have existed or may exist on this globe, or any globe,

All lives and deaths, all of the past, present, future,

This vast similitude spans them, and always has spann'd,

And shall forever span them and compactly hold and enclose them.

独自在夜晚的海滩上

独自在夜晚的海滩上,
年迈的海洋母亲来回摇晃着,唱着嘶哑的歌曲,
我看着星光闪烁,思索着宇宙和未来的谱号。

一种无边的相似把万物相连,
所有的星球,成形的、未成形的,微小的、巨大的,恒星、卫星、行星,
所有空间的距离,不管多么遥远,
所有时间的距离,所有无生命的形态,
所有灵魂,所有鲜活的肉体,无论它们自身或它们的世界多么迥异,
所有气体、液体、植物、矿物的进化过程,所有的游鱼和走兽,
所有民族、肤色、野蛮、文明、语言,
所有这个星球或是别的星球上曾经来过或仍然存在的身份,
所有生命和死亡,所有过去的、现在的、未来的,
这种无边的相似贯穿着它们,一直贯穿着,
并将永远贯穿着它们,并紧紧地拥抱着、包围着它们。

Beginning My Studies

Beginning my studies, the first step pleas'd me so much,
The mere fact, consciousness—these forms—the power of motion,
The least insect or animal—the senses—eyesight—love;
The first step, I say, aw'd me and pleas'd me so much,
I have hardly gone, and hardly wish'd to go, any farther,
But stop and loiter all the time, to sing it in extatic songs.

开始我的研究

开始了我的研究,第一步就让我心生欢喜,
客观的事实,主观的意识,这些形态,还有移动的能力,
最微不足道的昆虫或动物,感觉,视力,还有爱;
要我说,这第一步就让我赞叹不已、心生欢喜,
我还没有探索多深,也不指望探索多深,
但我整日都在驻足欣赏,用狂欢的曲子将它歌唱。

Music

I heard you, solemn-sweet pipes of the organ, as last Sunday morn I passed
  the church;
Winds of autumn!—as I walked the woods at dusk, I heard your
  long-stretched sighs, up above, so mournful;
I heard the perfect Italian tenor, singing at the opera—I heard the
  soprano in the midst of the quartette singing.
—Heart of my love! you too I heard, murmuring low, through one of the
  wrists around my head;
Heard the pulse of you, when all was still, ringing little bells last night
  under my ear.

音 乐

管风琴呵,当我上周六途经教堂的时候,我听见你的旋律了,如此庄严美妙;

秋日的风呵,当我在黄昏穿过树林的时候,我听见你的长叹了,如此高远忧伤;

我听见了完美的意大利男高音在剧院里歌唱,我听见了女高音在四重奏里歌唱。

我心上的人啊!我也听见了你,你的手腕轻挽着我的头,你的喃喃低语传到耳边;

昨晚当万籁俱寂的时候,我听见了你的脉搏,它像小小的铃铛在我的耳下摇晃。

Weave in, Weave in, My Hardy Life

Weave in! weave in, my hardy life!
Weave yet a soldier strong and full, for great campaigns to come;
Weave in red blood! weave sinews in, like ropes! the senses, sight weave in!
Weave lasting sure! weave day and night the weft, the warp, incessant weave! tire not!

(We know not what the use, O life! nor know the aim, the end — nor really aught we know;
But know the work, the need goes on, and shall go on — the death-envelop'd march of peace as well as war goes on;)
For great campaigns of peace the same, the wiry threads to weave;
We know not why or what, yet weave, forever weave.

编织进来吧,编织进来吧,我艰辛的生活

编织进来吧,编织进来吧,我艰辛的生活,
编织出一个强健又充实的战士,为加入伟大的战役而来,
编织进来鲜红的血液,编织进来坚韧如绳索的肌腱,
把所感和所见都编织进来吧,
不停地编织,没日没夜地编织,编织出纬线和经线,
不知疲倦,永无休止。

(我们并不清楚生活的意义,也不知道它的目的,我们对此一无所知,
但是我们明白我们的工作在继续也应该继续,以死亡封缄的和平行军在继续,战争也在继续),
为和平而战的伟大战役,丝线需要继续编织,
我们并不清楚编织的原因,也不知道编织的内容,但就是要编织,无休无止。

Song of Myself 1

I celebrate myself, and sing myself,
And what I assume you shall assume,
For every atom belonging to me as good belongs to you.

I loafe and invite my soul,
I lean and loafe at my ease observing a spear of summer grass.

My tongue, every atom of my blood, form'd from this soil, this air,
Born here of parents born here from parents the same, and their parents the same,
I, now thirty-seven years old in perfect health begin,
Hoping to cease not till death.

Creeds and schools in abeyance,
Retiring back a while sufficed at what they are, but

never forgotten,
I harbor for good or bad, I permit to speak at every hazard,
Nature without check with original energy.

自我之歌 1

我赞美自我,歌唱自我,

我所默认的一切对你也适合,

因为属于我的每一个原子同样属于你。

我在世间游荡并邀我的灵魂同往,

我俯下身来,悠闲地观察夏日的一片草叶。

我的舌头,我血液中的每一个原子,都由这里的土壤和空气孕育,

我生在这里,我的父母同样如此,我父母的父母也同样如此,

我如今三十七岁了,身体壮硕康健,

希望自己活力满满,一直到死去的那天。

教条和学派先放一旁,

稍事休整,满足于现状,但永不遗忘,

无论前方是福是祸,我愿乘风破浪,

笑纳自然的一切,那原初的力量。

By Broad Potomac's Shore

By broad Potomac's shore, again old tongue
(Still uttering, still ejaculating, canst never cease this babble?)
Again old heart so gay, again to you, your sense, the full flush spring
returning,
Again the freshness and the odours, again Virginia's summer sky,
pellucid blue and silver,
Again the forenoon purple of the hills,
Again the deathless grass, so noiseless soft and green,
Again the blood-red roses blooming.
Perfume this book of mine O blood-red roses!
Lave subtly with your waters every line Potomac!
Give me of you O spring, before I close, to put between its pages!
O forenoon purple of the hills, before I close, of you!
O deathless grass, of you!

宽阔的波托马克河岸边

宽阔的波托马克河岸边,又是那条古老的舌头

(仍然在诉说,仍然在奔涌,无休无止的潺潺水声?)

衰老的心再次感到快乐,再次因为你和对你的感觉,

明媚的春天回来了,

再次嗅到新鲜的气息,再次看到弗吉尼亚的夏日天空,

一片透明的蓝色和银色,

再次领略清晨的紫色山丘,

再次抚摸不死的草叶,如此静谧柔软的绿色,

再次感受血红玫瑰的怒放。

哦,血红玫瑰,让我的这本书散发你的芳香!

让你的水流细密地冲刷波托马克的每一条河岸线!

哦春天,在我闭合之前,把你自己献祭给我,夹在书页之间!

哦清晨的紫色山丘,在我闭合之前!

哦不死的草叶,在我离去之前!

William Wordsworth
[英国]威廉·华兹华斯
1770—1850

华兹华斯是英国浪漫主义文学的奠基人之一,与同时代的柯勒律治、骚赛一起被称为"湖畔派"诗人。他开创了清新朴实、情景交融的浪漫派诗歌风格,他的《抒情歌谣集·序言》被称为英国浪漫主义的宣言。

I Wandered Lonely as a Cloud

I wandered lonely as a cloud
That floats on high o'er vales and hills,
When all at once I saw a crowd,
A host, of golden daffodils;
Beside the lake, beneath the trees,
Fluttering and dancing in the breeze.

Continuous as the stars that shine
And twinkle on the milky way,
They stretched in never-ending line
Along the margin of a bay:
Ten thousand saw I at a glance,
Tossing their heads in sprightly dance.

The waves beside them danced; but they
Out-did the sparkling waves in glee:
A poet could not but be gay,
In such a jocund company:
I gazed—and gazed—but little thought

What wealth the show to me had brought:

For oft, when on my couch I lie
In vacant or in pensive mood,
They flash upon that inward eye
Which is the bliss of solitude;
And then my heart with pleasure fills,
And dances with the daffodils.

我仿佛一朵孤飞的流云

我仿佛一朵孤飞的流云
在山谷之间徘徊游荡，
美景刹那映入眼帘，
那是一簇金色水仙；
就在湖边，就在树下，
风中摇曳，舞姿翩翩。

它宛如一片璀璨的群星，
在银河两岸熠熠闪烁，
蔓延舒展永不止息，
沿着河岸步履不停：
一眼千朵，一眼万朵，
婀娜明媚，频频颔首。

水波潋滟，轻歌曼舞，
若论风姿，不及水仙：
诗人恰逢快乐的伴侣，
心中怎能不绽放欢颜：
我长久凝望，却未能体味

此情此景赐予我的财富:

每每当我,寂寞独卧,
百无聊赖,忧戚空落,
它们便在眼前浮现,
那正是独处的喜悦;
我的心便随水仙起舞,
再次充盈着幸福快乐。

A Complaint

There is a change—and I am poor;
Your love hath been, nor long ago,
A fountain at my fond heart's door,
Whose only business was to flow;
And flow it did; not taking heed
Of its own bounty, or my need.

What happy moments did I count!
Blest was I then all bliss above!
Now, for that consecrated fount
Of murmuring, sparkling, living love,
What have I? shall I dare to tell?
A comfortless and hidden well.

A well of love—it may be deep—
I trust it is,—and never dry:
What matter? if the waters sleep
In silence and obscurity.
—Such change, and at the very door
Of my fond heart, hath made me poor.

哀 怨

一切顷刻天翻地转,如今我委实可怜;
就在不久之前,
你的爱还是奔涌在我心门的清泉,
它终日所求便是汩汩流淌,
永远流淌,
不计得失,慷慨如常。

我曾经拥有多少欢愉的时刻!
胜过世间所有的情缘!
要知那汪神圣的泉水,
曾喃喃细语、光彩夺目、生机盎然,
我现在得到的是什么?哪还有勇气去诉说?
只剩一口冰冷的暗井相伴。

爱情的暗井或许深不见底,
我相信如此,它永不枯干:
然而又有何用?倘若
井水沉睡,缄默无声。
这样的落差,就在我的心门面前,
我实在可怜,只因爱人的情变。

I Travelled among Unknown Men

I travelled among unknown men,
In lands beyond the sea;
Nor, England! did I know till then
What love I bore to thee.

'Tis past, that melancholy dream!
Nor will I quit thy shore
A second time; for still I seem
To love thee more and more.

Among thy mountains did I feel
The joy of my desire;
And she I cherished turned her wheel
Beside an English fire.

Thy mornings showed, thy nights concealed,
The bowers where Lucy played;
And thine too is the last green field
That Lucy's eyes surveyed.

我在陌生的人群中孤独穿行

我在陌生的人群中孤独穿行,
飘洋过海,异乡凋零;
呵,英格兰!那时我才明了
我对你怀有的深情。

已成过往,那忧郁的梦!
我再不愿驶离你的海岸;
因为随着时间的流逝,
我爱你似乎更胜从前。

当我在你的山间游荡,
我曾深感内心的欢畅;
我爱的姑娘转动着纺车,
就在一处故土的壁炉旁。

朝朝暮暮,光影婆娑,
抚过露西曾嬉戏的楼阁;
你那碧绿无垠的田野
正是露西的双眼最终所见。

Most Sweet it is

Most sweet it is with unuplifted eyes
To pace the ground, if path be there or none,
While a fair region round the traveller lies
Which he forbears again to look upon;
Pleased rather with some soft ideal scene,
The work of Fancy, or some happy tone
Of meditation, slipping in between
The beauty coming and the beauty gone.
If Thought and Love desert us, from that day
Let us break off all commerce with the Muse:
With Thought and Love companions of our way,
Whate'er the senses take or may refuse,
The Mind's internal heaven shall shed her dews
Of inspiration on the humblest lay.

最为甜蜜的事情

最为甜蜜的事情就是低垂着眼帘

阔步向前,哪管前方有路没路,

纵然美景就在旅人身边,

他也忍住不昂首四顾;

而是更青睐温柔的理想画面,

幻觉的杰作,抑或沉思的乐土。

在美的造访和美的消逝之间

自由穿梭,悠悠然然。

倘若思想和爱情背弃了我们,从那日起

我们只能斩断与缪斯所有的联系:

假如思想和爱情依然陪伴身边,

无论理智接纳或是舍弃,

内心的天堂也会降下甘露,

把灵感赋予最朴拙的诗篇。

It is a Beauteous Evening, Calm and Free

It is a beauteous evening, calm and free,

The holy time is quiet as a Nun

Breathless with adoration; the broad sun

Is sinking down in its tranquility;

The gentleness of heaven broods o'er the Sea;

Listen! the mighty Being is awake,

And doth with his eternal motion make

A sound like thunder—everlastingly.

Dear child! dear Girl! that walkest with me here,

If thou appear untouched by solemn thought,

Thy nature is not therefore less divine:

Thou liest in Abraham's bosom all the year;

And worshipp'st at the Temple's inner shrine,

God being with thee when we know it not.

那是一个美丽的夜晚,静谧而自由

那是一个美丽的夜晚,静谧而自由,

神圣的时刻,如修女一般沉默

因敬慕而屏息;辽阔的太阳

正在宁静中悄悄地沉落;

天堂的温柔笼罩着大海;

听!那伟大的生命正在苏醒,

他永恒的脉动迸发出

雷霆般的轰鸣——亘古未变,通往永恒。

亲爱的孩子!亲爱的姑娘!与我同路的人呐,

假如你看似尚未开悟灵通,

你的本性也不会因此少了虔诚:

一年到头你都躺在亚伯拉罕的怀里;

你在圣堂的内殿里朝拜,

即使我们毫不知晓,上帝也与你同行。

William Butler Yeats
[爱尔兰] 威廉·巴特勒·叶芝

1865—1939

爱尔兰诗人叶芝被公认为二十世纪最伟大的诗人之一。他执着地强调自己的爱尔兰身份,在自己的诗歌和戏剧作品中也融入了许多爱尔兰特色的传奇故事和人物。他写下了许多"最美丽的诗篇",在英语诗歌界广为传颂。

When You Are Old

When you are old and grey and full of sleep,
And nodding by the fire, take down this book,
And slowly read, and dream of the soft look
Your eyes had once, and of their shadows deep;

How many loved your moments of glad grace,
And loved your beauty with love false or true,
But one man loved the pilgrim soul in you,
And loved the sorrows of your changing face;

And bending down beside the glowing bars,
Murmur, a little sadly, how Love fled
And paced upon the mountains overhead
And hid his face amid a crowd of stars.

当你迟暮

当你迟暮,发丝斑白,神思不明,
壁炉边打盹,请拿出这部诗集,
徐徐朗读,遥想你那双眼昔日的柔意,
重温它们当年深邃的阴影;

无数人爱你青春洋溢的时刻,
倾慕你的容颜,虚情或真心,
唯有一人爱你那虔诚的灵魂,
爱你那风霜的脸上刻满的寂寞;

你弯下腰来,在炉火映照的栏杆旁,
呢喃爱情的消逝,黯然独自神伤,
在头顶的群山上爱也曾来回徜徉,
璀璨的星空里却藏起了他的模样。

The Lake Isle of Innisfree

I will arise and go now, and go to Innisfree,
And a small cabin build there, of clay and wattles made;
Nine bean-rows will I have there, a hive for the honey-bee,
And live alone in the bee-loud glade.

And I shall have some peace there, for peace comes dropping slow,
Dropping from the veils of the morning to where the cricket sings;
There midnight's all a glimmer, and noon a purple glow,
And evening full of the linnet's wings.

I will arise and go now, for always night and day
I hear lake water lapping with low sounds by the shore;
While I stand on the roadway, or on the pavements grey,
I hear it in the deep heart's core.

茵尼斯弗利岛

我即将动身,前往茵尼斯弗利岛,
在那里搭一座小屋,用黏土和竹篱;
我要养一箱蜜蜂,种九排豆角,
独居在蜜蜂喧闹的树林里。

我将在那儿得到安宁,它缓缓入场,
它来自拂晓的薄雾,也来自蟋蟀的歌唱;
子夜是一抹微光,正午是紫色骄阳,
傍晚则四处翻飞着红雀的翅膀。

我即将动身,因为我总是日日夜夜
听见湖水拍岸的喃喃低语;
当我站在公路或人行道,心情酸涩,
我听闻它在灵魂的深处倾诉。

The Travail of Passion

When the flaming lute-thronged angelic door is wide;
When an immortal passion breathes in mortal clay;
Our hearts endure the scourge, the plaited thorns, the way
Crowded with bitter faces, the wounds in palm and side,
The vinegar-heavy sponge, the flowers by Kedron stream;
We will bend down and loosen our hair over you,
That it may drop faint perfume, and be heavy with dew,
Lilies of death-pale hope, roses of passionate dream.

受 难

当熊熊燃烧的天使之门在琴瑟齐鸣中大敞；
当不死的激情在现世的泥泞里面残喘；
我们的心忍受着鞭打，缠绕的荆棘，路上
挤满痛苦的面庞，手掌和侧肋布满创伤，
又像浸透酸楚的海绵，汲沦谷溪流边的花朵；
我们将俯身用头发将你遮住，
它也许会散发淡淡的幽香，沉甸甸盈满露珠，
如死亡的百合只有渺茫的希望，又如春梦里的玫瑰
朵朵。

注：汲沦谷（Kedron），《圣经》中地名。

Down by the Salley Gardens

Down by the salley gardens my love and I did meet;
She passed the salley gardens with little snow-white feet.
She bid me take love easy, as the leaves grow on the tree;
But I, being young and foolish, with her would not agree.

In a field by the river my love and I did stand,
And on my leaning shoulder she laid her snow-white hand.
She bid me take life easy, as the grass grows on the weirs;
But I was young and foolish, and now am full of tears.

漫步柳园

漫步柳园,我的挚爱和我曾经相遇;
她雪白的小脚往柳园款款走去。
她劝我把求爱的热切放轻松,像树上长绿叶;
当时我年轻又愚蠢,无法与她心绪相通。

河边草地,我的挚爱和我曾经相守,
在我前倾的肩头她放下雪白的小手。
她要我把生活的执念放轻松,像堤坝上生野草;
当时我年轻又愚蠢,如今只有泪水滔滔。

The Cat and the Moon

The cat went here and there

And the moon spun round like a top,

And the nearest kin of the moon,

The creeping cat, looked up.

Black Minnaloushe stared at the moon,

For, wander and wail as he would,

The pure cold light in the sky

Troubled his animal blood.

Minnaloushe runs in the grass

Lifting his delicate feet.

Do you dance, Minnaloushe, do you dance?

When two close kindred meet.

What better than call a dance?

Maybe the moon may learn,

Tired of that courtly fashion,

A new dance turn.

Minnaloushe creeps through the grass

From moonlit place to place,

The sacred moon overhead

Has taken a new phase.
Does Minnaloushe know that his pupils
Will pass from change to change,
And that from round to crescent,
From crescent to round they range?
Minnaloushe creeps through the grass
Alone, important and wise,
And lifts to the changing moon
His changing eyes.

猫与月亮

猫四处游走,

月亮如陀螺般转圈,

月亮的近亲,

那只爬行的猫,抬头望天。

黑色的蜜娜露什盯着如银的月色

随意地走动与嚎叫,

夜空中清冷的光

让他血液里的兽性被搅扰。

蜜娜露什在草地上奔跑,

抬起他灵巧的小脚。

你跳舞么,蜜娜露什,你跳舞么?

当两个近亲相遇,

还有什么比共舞更妙?

也许月亮已厌倦了宫廷的舞步,

将学会一种

新潮的转舞。

蜜娜露什在草丛里爬行,

在月光的沐浴下从一处到另一处,

头顶那轮圣洁的月亮

已经呈现出新的模样。
蜜娜露什是否知道
他的瞳仁也跟着不断变幻,
由圆变缺,
又从缺变圆?
蜜娜露什在草丛里爬行,
孤孤单单,骄傲又聪明,
然后对着变幻的月亮
抬起他变幻的双眼。